1949
February
CHICAGO

I was born to Reverend Charles and Arthric Spivey. Aunt Mary and Uncle J.C. waited all night for me to come—on February 14. But YOU knew I wasn't coming until the fifteenth. I was the youngest of five. YOU knew my older brothers and sisters would grow up, move away, and I would become big sister to nine more babies. YOU knew Daddy and Mommy would give me a blessing I would recite all my life: "Blessed are the pure in heart, for they shall see God" (Matthew 5:8)

–JSG

You See Me, God
Text and illustrations © 2020 by Jan Spivey Gilchrist. All rights reserved.

Requests for permission to quote from this book should be directed to: Permissions Department, Our Daily Bread Publishing, PO Box 3566, Grand Rapids, MI 49501 or contact us by email at permissionsdept@odb.org.

Library of Congress Cataloging-in-Publication Data available upon request.

Interior design by Kris Nelson/StoryLook Design

ISBN: 978-1-62707-938-9

Printed in China

21 22 23 24 25 26 27 / 8 7 6 5 4 3 2

You See Me, God

Inspired by Psalm 139

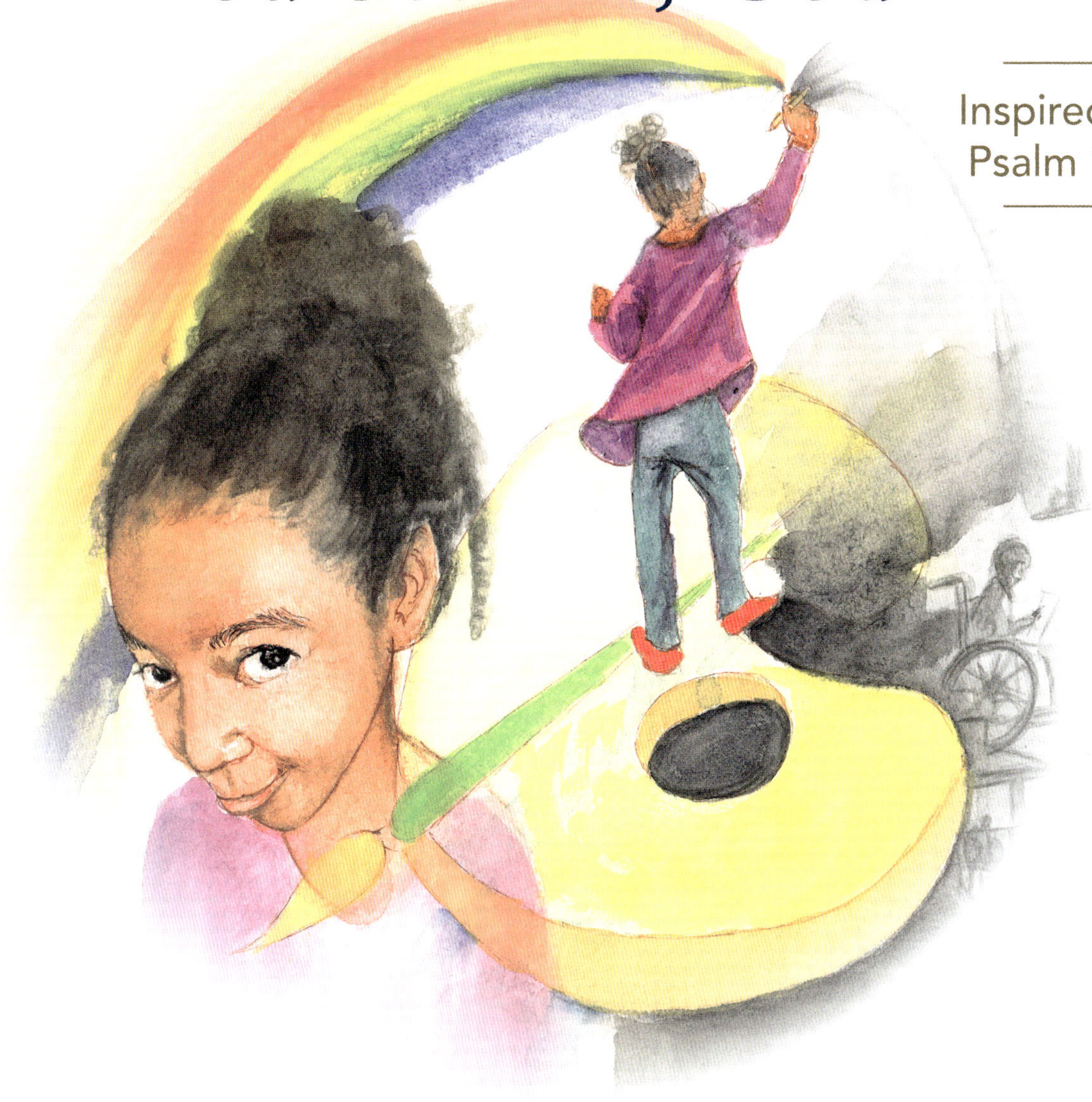

Jan Spivey Gilchrist

YOU made me ME.

In Your image.

Black.

And beautiful.

And blessed.

Full of Your powerful promise.

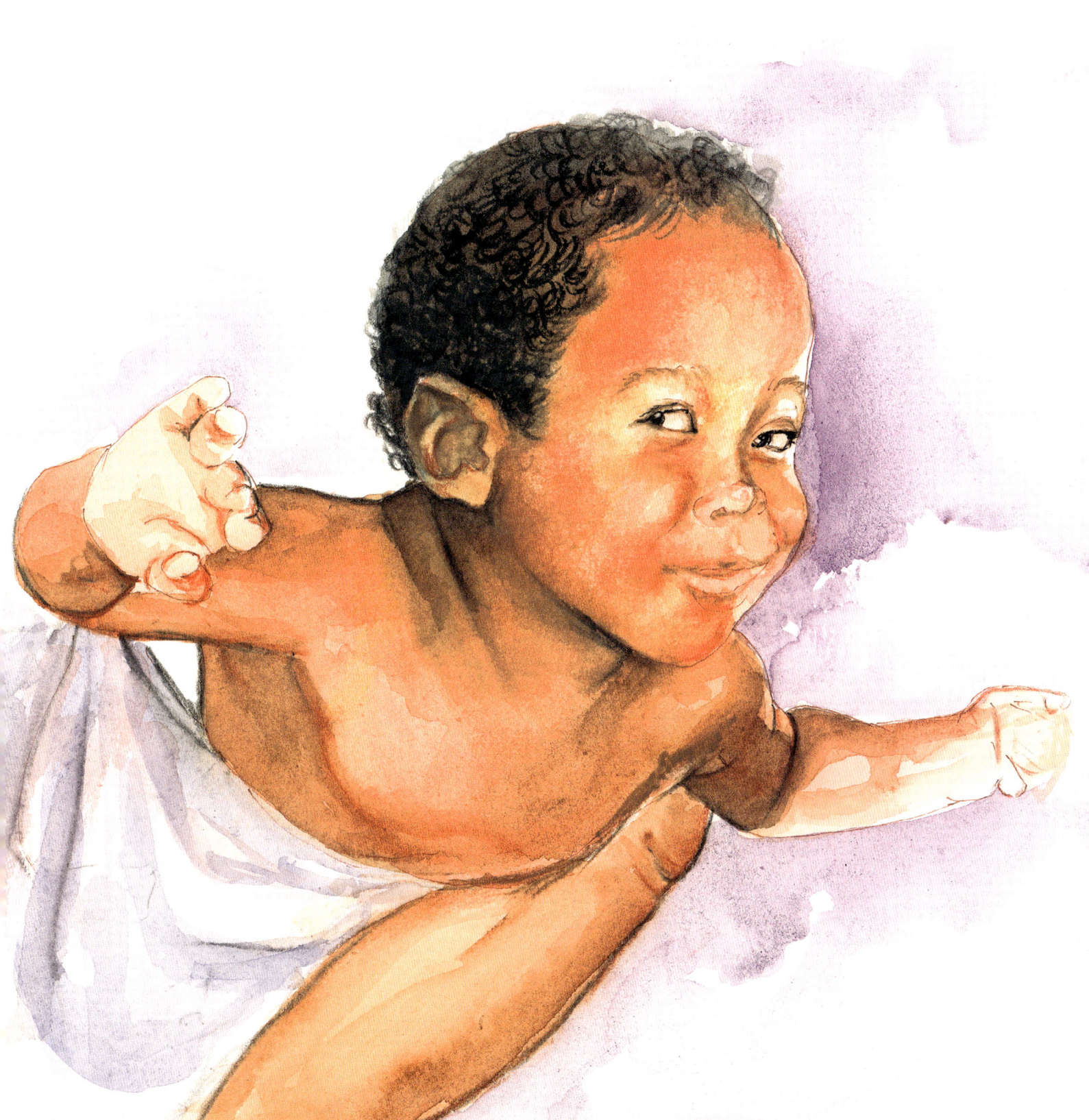

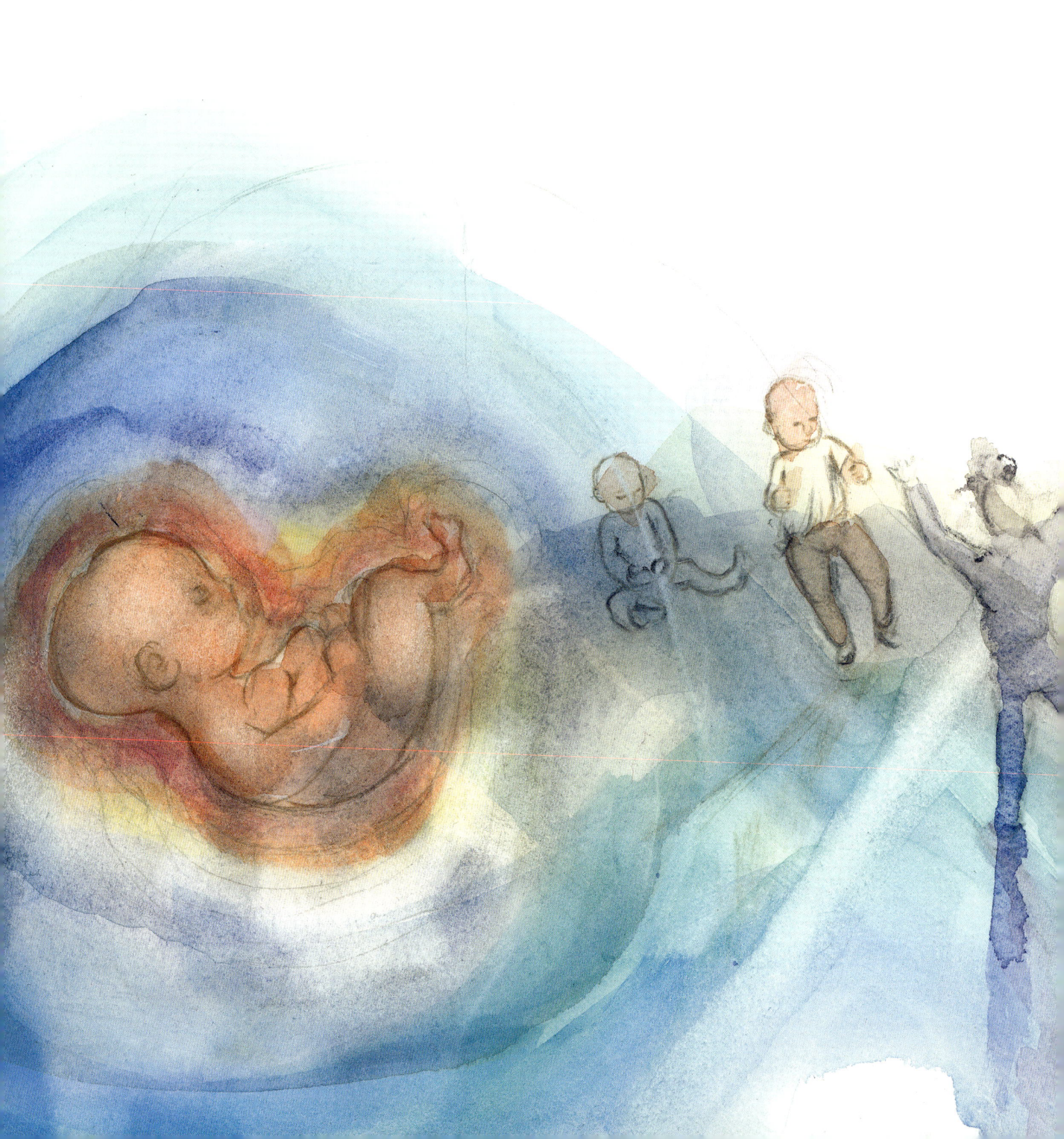

YOU knew me before I knew myself.
YOU saw me tight like a balloon inside my mother.

Ready to fill the world with my colors.

YOU know what I love and what I fear.
YOU see me everywhere.
I cannot hide from YOU.

YOU saw me when I cracked
and broke into tiny pieces.
YOU knew my legs would break.
YOU knew I would fall.

YOU found me when I was scared and lost.
YOU knew how to help me.
YOU knew I would one day stand tall.

YOU heard me call out from my darkness.
YOU knew that I would.
YOU see me everywhere…
and YOU are always with me.

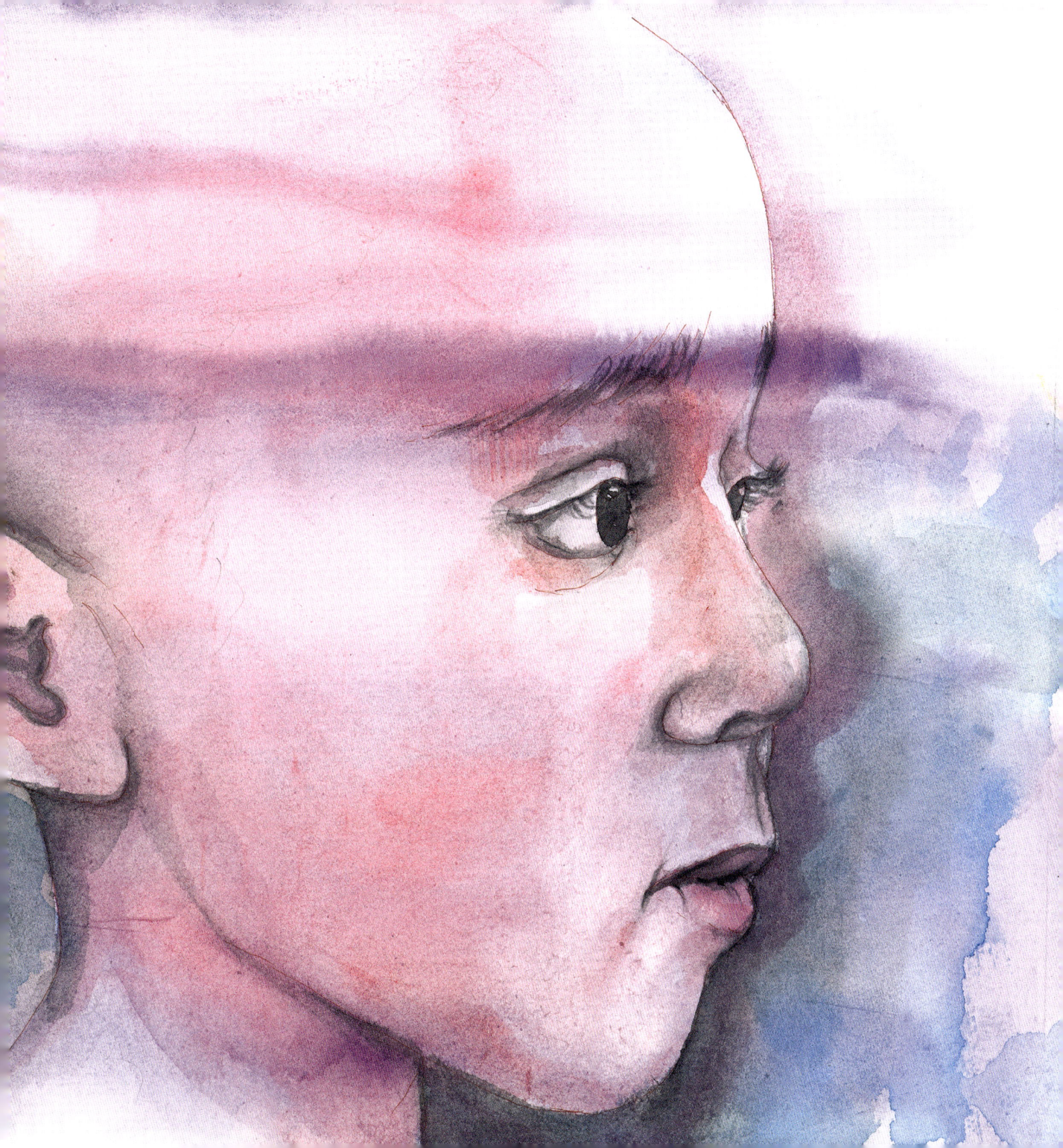

YOU are always with me.

YOU lifted me.
YOU will guide me.

YOU help me share Your love with others.

Your thoughts are wonderful to me.

I live my life in PEACE every day.

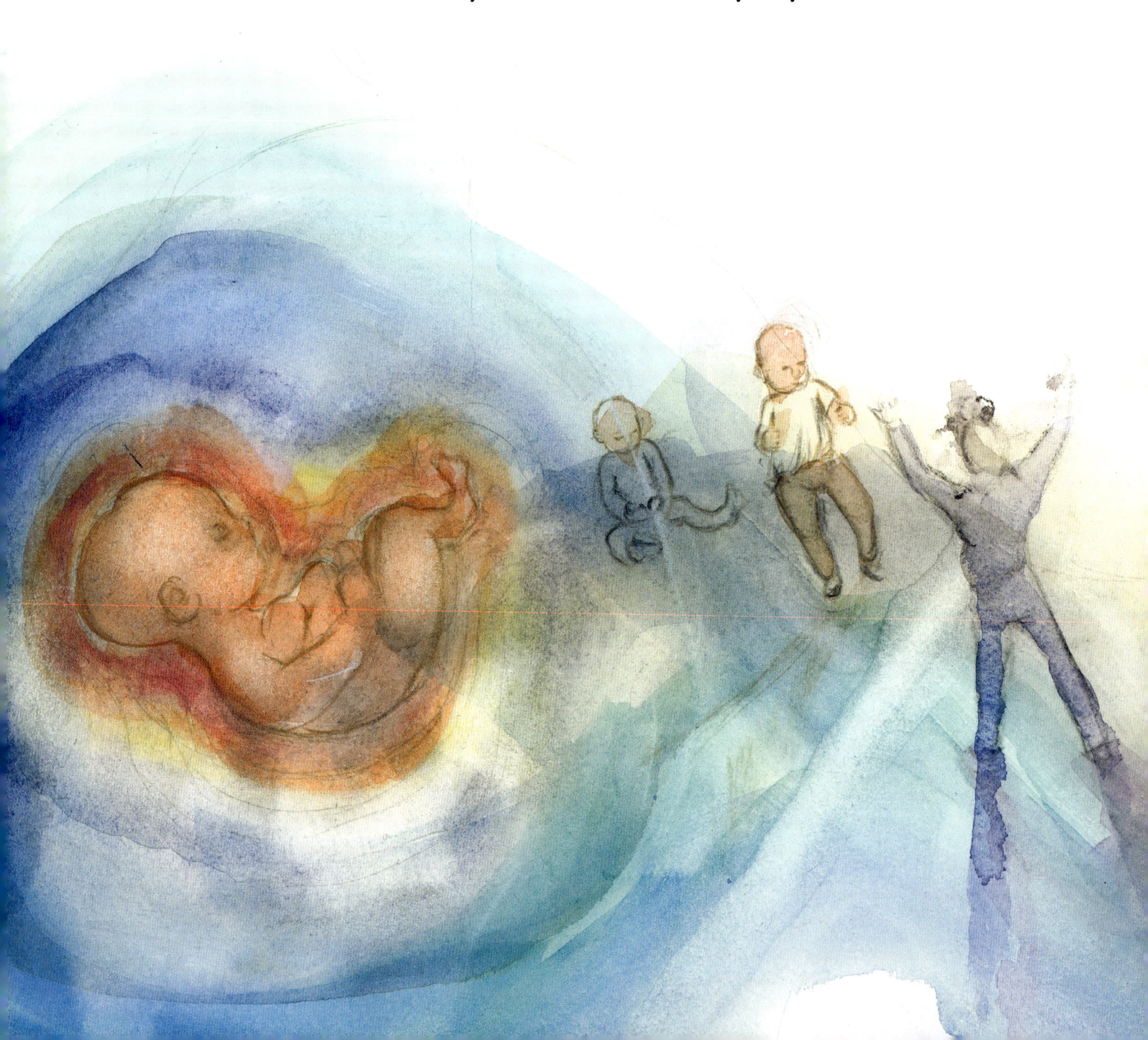

Because I know YOU see me.

Lord…

You see my heart.

You know what I think.

You know all about me.

You see me everywhere.

You know what I say.

You know how I live.

You created me inside my mother's body.

How You have made me is wonderful.

Help me live in the right way.

Paraphrase of selected verses from Psalm 139

When my family sat down to eat together, we always "blessed" the table.

Each of us picked a Bible verse.

Mine was Matthew 5:8:

"Blessed are the pure in heart: for they shall see God."

I have repeated this verse my entire life. It is always a reminder…

You see me, know me, and are with me.